T0199007

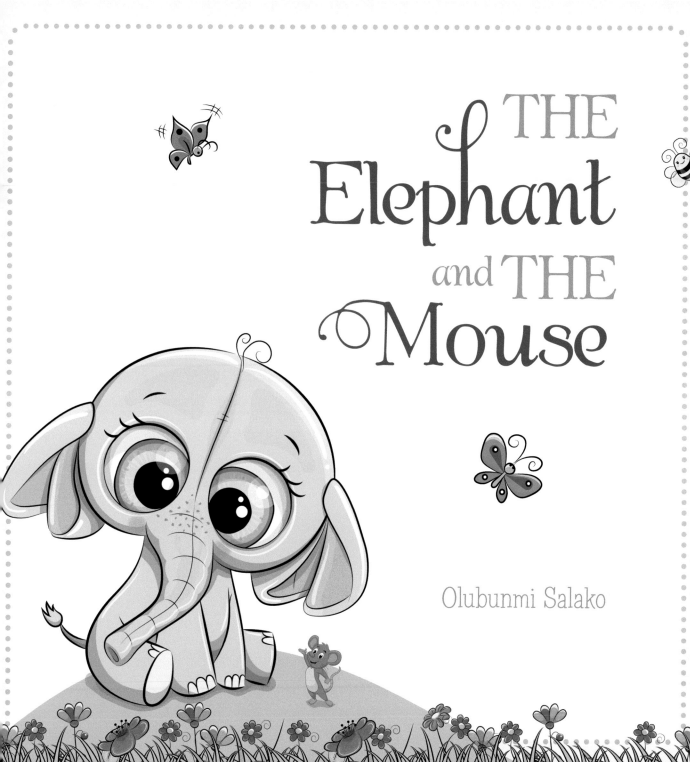

THE Elephant and THE Mouse

Olubunmi Salako

AuthorHouse™
1663 Liberty Drive
Bloomington, IN 47403
www.authorhouse.com
Phone: 1 (800) 839-8640

Because of the dynamic nature of the Internet, any web addresses or links contained in this book may have changed
since publication and may no longer be valid. The views expressed in this work are solely those of the author and do not
necessarily reflect the views of the publisher, and the publisher hereby disclaims any responsibility for them.

Any people depicted in stock imagery provided by Getty Images are models,
and such images are being used for illustrative purposes only.
Certain stock imagery © Getty Images.

This book is printed on acid-free paper.

ISBN: 978-1-7283-5370-8 (sc)
ISBN: 978-1-7283-5369-2 (e)

Print information available on the last page.

Published by AuthorHouse 06/27/2020

authorHOUSE®

Long ago in the animal kingdom, the Elephant paraded himself as the king of the jungle contrary to the widespread belief that Lion occupied that position. His belief was based on his size and strength.

Truly, the Elephant is one of the biggest animals in
the jungle and he is also an intelligent animal.

The Elephant was always prepared to crush any animal who dared
crossed the line. Whenever the Lion wanted to assert his authority
in the jungle, the Elephant was battle ready to challenge him.

The Mouse on the other hand is arguably the smallest animal in the jungle. He is a gentle animal that quietly moves around without calling attention to itself.

One day, the Mouse delivered ten new babies
(mice have many babies at a time).

She needed to enlarge her house to make room for her new arrivals. She started building her house using old papers, twigs, cardboard and leaves which she had collected earlier. She thought of what she could gather around to complete the job.

She had an idea.

The Elephant lived nearby, and she remembered she used the Elephant's dung in the past to pad her walls.

She therefore sent six of her older children to the field to get some Elephant's dung.

They set out.

The Elephant was chomping on the field when they arrived. They looked nearby to see if there were dungs, but found none.

They decided to move closer without being noticed. Just as they got to where the Elephant was, they noticed he was just defecating.

They rushed to collect some.

Accidentally, the dung landed on two Mice
and they were buried under it.

They got terribly anxious. They struggled to
free themselves to avoid suffocation.

The two Mice tried eating through the dung, unknown to
them; they were nibbling at the Elephant's foot. The Elephant
lifted his foot and accidentally landed on the Mice.

They were crushed to death.

The Jumbo Elephant flapped its ears, trumpeted and
walked away, not realising what had happened.

The remaining Mice scurried back home in sorrow.
They told their mother the sad news.

Mother Mouse was grief-stricken.

Without much of a doubt, she concluded the Elephant did it on
purpose as many animals believed that the Elephant was a big bully.

The next day, the Mouse decided to confront him.

The Elephant was at the other side of the field covering himself with dust to shield its skin from the sun.

The Mouse quietly approached him.

"Why did you kill my children yesterday?"
the Mouse asked from a distance.

"I don't know what you are talking about," replied the Elephant.

"Stop pretending," shouted the Mouse. "I sent six of my children out yesterday to get some of your dung and all you did was kill two of them for packing your waste." the Mouse snapped.

One would expect that the Elephant would show some empathy towards the Mouse for the loss of her children. At least he could explain that it was an accident.

No! instead he started his usual boasting as the strongest animal that a small animal like Mouse could not confront with a charge.

"Oh!" because of your size you think you can treat other animals like your dung?" the Mouse asked.

At this point the Mouse was shaking in anger.

She promised to show the Elephant that she may be small,
she knew how best to deal with bullies like him.

The Elephant ordered her to leave.

"Yes, I will leave but be assured that I shall be
back for you." the Mouse threatened.

The Elephant laughed at her scornfully.

"If you don't leave this minute, I will trample on you and you will die like your miserable children," the Elephant replied angrily.

"You see how big I am, even a drop of my dung is bigger than you." he teased.

The Mouse felt really humiliated and sad. She turned around and headed home.

She lost her sleep that night. She thought of the best way to handle the boastful Elephant.

WHAT SHOULD I DO?

She came up with a perfect plan.

The next day, she divided her children into two groups and gave them tasks to carry out. She warned them to be very cautious while at it. She later visited her friend, the Bee, to ask for her support in this battle.

They were all equipped to wage war against the Elephant for being so insensitive, callous and arrogant.

They went over their roles.

They decided to sneak to the field at sunset when the Elephant would have returned from the lake. The first group would nibble at the Elephant's feet to distract him so the other group could enter his trunk.

The Bee would enter his ears and eyes. (Bees
loved the water around Elephant's eyes).

They arrived just as the Elephant was returning from the lake
where he had had a good bath and a cool drink of water.

As soon as he settled down to have a nap, Mother Mouse and her troop
attacked. He didn't feel the nibbling at first because of his thick skin.

He did eventually.

He got up and moved his feet to dislodge himself from the Mice.

They followed him.

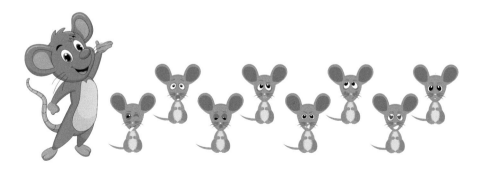

While still moving from one place to another, the other group climbed quietly into his trunk. Before he realised what was happening, the Bees entered his ears buzzing loudly, humming and stinging.

The Elephant went berserk.

He plodded across the field, trumpeting. He became agitated and aggressive that he tore down all the trees on his way.

The other animals heard the loud noise, and they
came out to see what was happening.

The animals in the jungle were sore afraid to see Jumbo Elephant in
such distress. Those he had bullied in the past were secretly happy.

He ran very fast thinking that would
help him get rid of the pests. He roared
louder and rumbled like thunder.

He fell on the grass, kicked, rolled, and raised his trunk
up and down. He got up and flapped his ears.

The other animals ran in different directions making loud sounds.

The Tigers growled, the Bats screeched, the Antelopes snorted, the Chimpanzees screamed, the Cows mooed, the Ducks quacked, the Giraffes bleated, the Rhinoceros bellowed, the Chickens clucked, the Horses neighed and Lion the king roared.

There was absolute chaos in the animal kingdom.

The Elephant jumped up and down and landed on the tail of the snake that was hiding in the grass. The snake hissed and crawled slowly down to the lake.

After a while, the Mouse came to the Elephant.

"Did you enjoy that?" she asked mockingly.
"Now you realise size doesn't matter."

"I'm sorry!" the Elephant interrupted.

"I will never treat you like that again." he promised.

"I'm so sorry," he begged again.

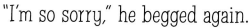

The Mouse laughed.

She was happy she taught the Elephant a good lesson.

"He who laughs last, laughs best," she quipped.

The Mouse then ordered her children to come out of the Elephant's trunk. She also begged the Bees to vacate his ears and eyes.

They obeyed.

The Elephant felt a great relief as soon as the last rodent exited.

He ran as fast as his fat legs could carry him fearing another attack.

The Elephant was put in his place once and for all. He could have settled this kindly if he had apologised to Mother Mouse for the accident. After all, it was an accident.

Mother Mouse thanked her friend, for standing by her and supporting her to teach the big bully a lesson.

She proudly led her children back home. The Bee also led her swarm back to the hive buzzing happily as they went.

The Elephant was ashamed and blamed himself for
looking down on the Mouse because of her size.

What a lesson to learn! He learnt in a hard
way to always treat others right.

He couldn't roam the field for several days because of the disgrace he
suffered in the hands of a small animal which other animals preyed on.

The Elephant became humble and gentle after what had happened.
He made friends with other animals who he used to snub. Many
animals were attracted to him because of his change of attitude.

Birds became his best friends. They came regularly to play with him. They would land on his back singing to him while he grazed on the field.

Peace was restored in the kingdom as there was no more argument about who was the greatest. The other animals were no longer afraid of being bullied. They owed that to Mother Mouse who stood up to the bully.

Since that time, the buzzing of the Bee caused the Elephant to move far away. And whenever he noticed the appearance of the Mouse, he would take off in the opposite direction.

Printed in the United States
By Bookmasters